Sophie Washington
My BFF

By
Tonya Duncan Ellis

Other Books by
Tonya Duncan Ellis

Table of Contents

Chapter 1

Pleasure Pier

My mom says a good way to finish something I hate doing, like eating Brussels sprouts, is to get on with it, and count backward from ten until I'm done. I tried it last week after she made me apologize for calling my brother Nugget Head. It was a *teensy* bit easier.

But what's happening right now is so terrible that I silently count down all the way from one hundred, and squeeze my eyes shut.

"Ninety-nine, ninety-eight, ninety-seven, ninety-six…"

"Isn't this great, Sophie?!" Chloe interrupts my thoughts and grabs my hand as the attendant snaps us in our seats. "It's so pretty up here. Look down!"

I peek open one eye and spy huge waves splashing under us as our cart creaks up the track. Brightly colored umbrellas dot the sand below like Skittles, and I suck in the warm sea breeze to calm myself. I can't believe I let my best friend convince me to get on the Killer Whale, the biggest roller coaster at Pleasure Pier.

Our science class is on a day trip to Galveston Bay, about an hour from Houston, where we live. We spent the morning looking at turtles, shells, and crabs on the beach. Our visit to the amusement park is an extra "treat."

"This is going to be epic!" shouts Chloe, as we inch higher up the hill. She raises both arms in the air. I grip the handle on the roller coaster seat so tightly my knuckles are sore. Sea gulls fly above us through cottony clouds, without a care in the world. If only I could be so calm. I'm wet-your-pants scared right now.

"Have the Time of Your Life," says a sign outside the entrance, with palm trees on either side. *Yeah, right.*

The only reason I'm not at the carnival games is because I want to spend time with my BFF, Chloe. We've been friends since we shared a swing in kindergarten, and we do everything together, like cheer for our school and play on the tennis team. She's taller and noisier than I am, but somehow, we belong together, like chips and salsa.

Chloe isn't in any of my classes this year. During free periods she gets special tutoring for her dyslexia. Don't ask me what dyslexia means exactly, but she's not so great at spelling and takes twice as long as the rest of us to do her school work.

Chloe's been talking about riding the Killer Whale since we were too short to be allowed on roller coasters. I'd do anything for my best friend, and I didn't want to look like a chicken, so I faced my fear.

Looking back, I still can't believe I got in line when Chloe begged. The Killer Whale is a perfect name for that ride. Carts race up and down the grayish blue rails like they're on a speed track, and then drop down huge hills.

"That's what I'm talking about!" Toby, the cutest boy in the sixth grade, stood in front of us in line with his mouth open. "Forget about the baby rides; I want to ride this one the whole time we're here."

"This is so cool!" Nathan, Toby's buddy for the field trip, gave him a high five. "and since there are two tracks, we shouldn't have to wait long to get on."

The crowded line came to a standstill and we continued to talk.

"Hey, Sophie, did you start that poetry assignment for English class?" Toby edged around Chloe. "Can you help me with it at school tomorrow? I need to get an A or B to raise my grade."

"You read the poem yet?" said Nathan, pausing the video game he was playing on his phone and also looking my way. "I can't figure it out."

"Why didn't you ask me what I think about the poem?" asked Chloe with a frown.

"Well, ah, I didn't think you were doing the same work," said Toby.

Her lips curled, and I braced myself.

Chloe is super sweet most of the time, but act like she's not as smart as someone else, and she changes from cuddly kitten to ferocious tiger.

"As a matter of fact, I *am* doing the same work," she said, wrapping her arms around her chest. "Just because I go to a tutor sometimes doesn't mean I don't know what's going on. I still have the same English assignments as you guys."

"I don't think he meant that, Chloe," I said.

"Yeah, yeah, everybody knows you're the spelling champion, while I'm the sixth-grade dummy," said Chloe.

"Now wait a minute…" I said.

Ahhhhh!

My braids were blown back by the air from a roller coaster cart. The line started to move again, and Valentina, another of our good friends, pulled out her cell phone. "Get closer, guys, I want to get picture of us in front of the Killer Whale."

We all leaned in. Chloe, who looks like a tween model, shook her shiny black curls and flashed a bright smile for the camera. I hoped my two braids weren't sticking up.

"Let me see." Valentina's field trip partner, Mariama, peered down at the picture, and giggled. "Your eyes are all bugged out, Sophie!"

"OMG!" Chloe put her hand over her mouth to hold in her laugh.

I grabbed for the phone. "Delete that, Valentina!"

"No problemo, I'll take another one," she said.

The people in back pushed us, so we had to go forward.

"Come on, y'all! The line's moving." Chloe eased us closer to the Killer Whale, and I forgot about the embarrassing picture.

I wanted to ride the Killer Whale as much as a fish wants to be hooked on a line. A couple of months ago, I threw up at the top of a giant slide at a school festival. But I didn't want to look like a scaredy-cat in front of Chloe and my other friends.

Now I'm strapped into this lunchbox on wheels with no way out. We move faster, and I begin to count again.

"Ninety-five, ninety-four, ninety-three, ninety-two…"

"Here we go!"

Chapter 2

Bad and Bougie

"How was the field trip?" Mom asks as soon as she picks me up after school.

"Can I get some of that medicine in the pink bottle when we get home?" I answer.

"Isn't that for when you have the runs?" asks my little brother, Cole. "Ewww, Sophie has diarrhea! Did you know diarrhea is hereditary? It runs it your jeans."

"Then that means you have it too, Poop Head!" I say, leaning over the car seat to hit his boxy Afro with my notebook.

"That's enough you two," says Mom, raising her voice. "Cut it out. How do you know what 'hereditary' and 'genes' mean anyway, Cole? You're only eight years old."

"We learned about it in science class," he answers. "You get genes from your parents that tell your hair color, eye color, height, and other things that make you who you are."

"Impressive," says my mother. "I guess all this money we're spending on private school is paying off."

"Really, Mom?" I say. "Cole was being totally gross

with me, and you didn't even say anything about it."

"You're right, sweetie," she answers. "That was inappropriate of you to speak to your sister that way, Cole. Please apologize."

"Soorrry," he says with a smirk.

"He's so fake," I say and roll my eyes. "I could really be sick, and nobody cares."

"Well, what happened?" asks Mom. "Did you eat too many funnel cakes, or try those greasy fried Oreos?"

"No, I rode the Killer Whale and some other big rides, and afterwards my stomach hurt." I rub my midsection.

"Wow!" exclaims Cole. "Jacob says that ride is dope. I'll bet that Bougie friend of yours, Chloe, dared you. You're too much of a 'fraidy cat to ride a roller coaster."

"Be quiet, Big Head." I cut my eyes at him.

"Here we go again with the name calling," says Mom, as we pull up to our driveway, and our two-story house comes into view. "Keep it up and I'm sending both of you to your rooms until dinner."

"Yes, Ma'am," we both answer and get quiet. When my mother says she's going to do something, she means it.

After we set our books on the desk near the kitchen, Cole grabs some cookies and milk and settles down to do his homework. It's warm and sunny outside, and if I wasn't sick, I'd take our dog for a walk. My dad jokes that our neighborhood in the suburbs of Houston is like Disneyland because all the homes are beautiful with perfectly cut lawns and flowers. I'd say it's more like the Animal Planet channel because we have real, live alligators around here, and wild pigs and deer run through the streets after dark.

Mom gives me a spoonful of medicine for my upset stomach and places a cuddly throw blanket over my legs. I don't want to admit it, but Cole is right. I wouldn't have gotten on the Killer Whale if Chloe hadn't been my field trip buddy. We usually get along great, but lately, she's been acting funny. After we got off the roller coaster, I told her I was dizzy, but she kept daring me to get on other rides. By the time we left the park my head hurt too. If she was sick, I would have sat down on a bench with her. Maybe she didn't realize how bad I felt. We're besties, and she'd never do anything to hurt me.

I start to get warm under the blanket, so I sit up. My stomach is not queasy anymore.

"Come here, Poochie." I call over our Portuguese Water Dog, Bertram, for a belly rub. Loving the attention, he turns his head and licks my cheek.

"How ya doing sweet boy?" I say in a baby voice.

Bertram sticks out his tongue, and his mouth curves up like he's smiling, while I stroke his black, curly fur.

Suddenly, my cell phone pings, and I press the on button.

This pic of u is sooo funny! reads a text message from Chloe.

Attached is the photo Valentina took right before we got on the Killer Whale. I look like the "before" picture in a makeover show and my cute friends look like the "after."

"Valentina told me she would delete this!" I scroll through the comments from half the sixth-grade class.

What's up with Sophie?

LOL. Check out her eyes!

☺ She looks cray cray!

9

This needs to come down, NOW.

"What should I do? Let me call Valentina!"

As I hit the button on my phone to send her a message, I notice the name on the top of the picture that shows who posted it.

Chloe Hopkins

Chapter 3

911

I drop my cell phone onto the couch, and put my head down on my forehead for a minute. I must look pretty sad because Bertram comes over and stares with big eyes. I'm not sure what to do. Chloe is my best friend. Why would she send around an ugly picture of me and laugh about it?

I don't want to let my mother know, because she might lecture me, or worse yet, tell my dad, who would take my phone because he thinks I'm too young to have one anyway.

Cole is too silly to understand what's going on. He'd probably just say some corny joke, like, "Don't worry what other people say, believe in your selfie."

Maybe Chloe didn't mean anything by it. She doesn't realize how silly it makes me look.

But Chloe knew that picture made me look bad. She said so in her message. I can't figure it out. Is she mad at me? Did I do something wrong? There's no way I'd put a picture like that of her on the Internet. How did she get it in the first place?

My chest tightens.

"Feeling better, sweetie?" My mother comes into the family room from the kitchen. "I see you're sitting up."

"Yeah, my stomach doesn't hurt anymore." I pick at the fluff on the tan, knit throw cover. "What's for dinner?"

"You kids act like I'm a walking refrigerator," Moms says with a laugh. "I've been helping Cole with his homework and lost track of time. I think we'll do something quick and easy like spaghetti tonight."

"Yay! I love spaghetti!" cheers Cole from across the room.

"Sounds good to me, Mom."

"Do you have homework?" Mom asks. "You've been lying around here for the past hour."

"Our teachers didn't give us any since we were on the field trip all day."

"Lucky," says Cole. "We had two whole worksheets for math."

"You're in the second grade." I twist my mouth. "How hard could it be? It was probably 2+2=4."

"Ha! Ha! You think you're so funny."

"Your brother works as hard on his schoolwork as you do, Sophie," says Mom. "You ought to be nicer to him."

"She can't help it, she's just a Meanie." Cole pouts.

"Whatever." I flip my hand. I stand up from the brown leather couch.

"Well, I can tell you are feeling like your regular self," says Mom. "How about unloading the dishwasher before I start cooking?"

"Um. My tummy still hurts a little bit." I bend over from my waist.

"Look at her, Mom. She's acting!" says Cole.

"Since you have so much to say, why don't you help your sister?"

I smile and stick my tongue out at him, when Mom leaves the area. He ignores me and rushes to get half the dishes put up so he can beat me back to the family room and hog the TV.

Fighting with Cole makes me forget about the drama with my friends for a few minutes, but I need to figure out what is going on. Maybe I'll call Valentina.

Chapter 4

Picture Perfect

"Why'd you give Chloe that ugly picture of me?" I demand as soon as Valentina picks up the line.

"What are you talking about?" she answers.

I sit on the edge of my fluffy pink bedspread and tap my foot on the carpet as I speak. My fish, Goldy, swims peacefully around his bowl on my dresser. I wish my life was so drama-free.

"Chloe sent the picture you took of all of us by the Killer Whale," I say. "You told me you'd delete it."

"I did delete it on the bus back to school," she says. "There's no way I'd keep a picture of you looking that goofy. Maybe Chloe didn't realize you'd get this mad about it."

I stand up and pace the floor.

"If you got rid of the picture than how did Chloe get it?"

"I dunno, we were all playing a game on my phone on the bus. Maybe she copied it then."

Knowing that Chloe copied the picture on purpose makes me feel worse. Is she really my friend? I want to ask her about it, but I'm scared. Did she mean to hurt me?

"Everybody in sixth grade and probably the whole middle school is laughing at me now."

"I'm really sorry, Sophie," says Valentina. "You do look funny in the picture, but it's not that bad. If we get Chloe to delete it, everyone will probably forget about it."

"I guess so," I answer.

"Hey, my grandma's calling me for dinner. I gotta get off the phone," says Valentina. "Want me to ask Chloe to delete the picture for you?"

"No, I'll do it," I say. "Talk to you later."

I press the off button on my phone, look down at Chloe's text, and sit back down on my bed. My hand shakes as I press her phone number. I don't know what to say, and my mouth feels like it's filled with hour-old bubblegum. The phone rings five times before going to voice mail. I text Chloe.

Lol that pic is funny, but can you delete it?

I stare at the phone for a couple of minutes for a response, but she doesn't answer. Maybe she's doing homework. I'll check again later, I think, and walk back downstairs.

At dinner Cole talks nonstop about a fireman who visited his class.

"He sleeps in the firehouse sometimes, in case somebody has a fire in the nighttime, and he gets to drive a cool red truck."

"Sounds neat," says Mom. "I wondered why there was a fire truck in the parking lot when I picked you up."

"The fireman let us get in the front seat of the fire engine!" Cole waves his hand and almost knocks over his water glass. "I wish I could drive a fire truck."

"You never know, Son," says Dad. "You just might do that one day." He turns to me. "My other chatterbox has been quiet tonight. Anything interesting happen for you at school today, Sophie?"

"Nothing really." I twirl two pieces of spaghetti around my fork.

"She almost threw up riding the Killer Whale on her field trip," says Cole.

"Your mother told me your class went to Pleasure Pier," Dad says. "How was it?"

"Sophie crashed on the couch for a couple of hours after we got home," says Mom.

"I still am kind of tired," I say. "and I'm not really hungry. Can I go to my room?"

"You don't have a fever or anything do you, honey?" My mother gets up and puts her hand on my forehead. "Maybe you should go lie down. Where's your cell phone? Leave it with me before you go upstairs."

I get my phone from the desk in our family room and glance down at it before handing it over to my mother. There's still no message from Chloe. She's usually on her phone for at least an hour after school, so I know she had to see my text. What's going on?

Chapter 5

'Fraidy Cat

I'm so worried about the ugly picture at bedtime that I have a terrible dream. It's pitch-black, and I scream and hang tight in a roller coaster as it whizzes along the track. My cart stops with a jerk, and I can't see anything, but I smell body odor, pencil shavings, and dirty sneakers. I'm at the entrance of the Xavier Academy middle school. I fumble to unsnap my seat belt, and then stumble into a brightly lit hallway. Chloe and all my other friends huddle together by our lockers, looking at a sheet of paper. When they see me, everyone points and laughs. Posters are plastered all over the walls, and I walk closer to get a better view. They're copies of the Killer Whale picture with the words "fraidy cat" printed under my face. Suddenly, water floods the open door way, and a giant fish with teeth as tall as my brother Cole swims toward me. My friends keep laughing as I yell and run for my life.

"Sophie! Cole! Breakfast is ready!" A call from my mother wakes me up from the nightmare. We must be having cereal today because I don't smell any hot food cooking.

I have a crick in my neck from tossing and turning, and when I look in my mirror, my eyes are puffy. I stare at Goldy as he circles his fish bowl without blinking. I definitely don't want to go to school today.

Luckily, everybody thought I was sick when I went to bed last night, so getting my mom to let me stay home might not be too hard. I peek my head out of the door in my bedroom, and see a light on down the hallway.

"Hey, Cole!"

As I suspect, he's still in his room, probably reading through the guidebook that describes characters from that silly Video Rangers video game he loves.

I'm still sore from sleeping funny, so I roll my neck and do some jumping jacks.

"Good morning, Sophie." Cole skips into my room, happy for the invitation. Our dog, Bertram, follows and thumps his tail on the carpet. "Why aren't you going downstairs to eat?"

"I'm sick." I stop mid-jumping jack and whisper. "Can you tell Mom and Dad I may not be able to go to school?"

"Why can't you tell them yourself?" He puts his hands on his hips.

"Because I feel bad, silly!" I raise my voice. "Now go get Mom."

"What will you give me for telling Mom?" He moves toward the piggy bank on my dresser like it's pay day, and I throw a pillow at hm.

"Nothing, Creep. Just go!"

"You're not really sick!" he says. "I saw you bouncing around when I came in here. You just don't want to go to school."

Wondering what's keeping us from going down to pour his bowl of dog food, Bertram starts to whine and puts his paws on my knees.

"Mooom! Sophie's pretending to be sick and won't get dressed!" Cole yells.

"Get out of my room, you little Snitch!" I cry.

"What's going on up here?" my mother walks through the door. "You still feeling bad?"

"Yes." I slump on the edge of my bed.

"Well, you don't have a temperature." She feels my forehead. "Does anything else hurt you?"

"My head and my tummy."

"No fair, I want to stay home too." Cole frowns.

"I didn't say she was staying home," says Mom. "I'm trying to figure out what's going on. Let's get some toast and tea, to settle your stomach, Sophie, and we'll see if you feel any better."

I move slowly and slouch against my mother as we make our way down the staircase.

Downstairs, a tea kettle is heating on the stove and cereal bowls are already on the counter for us to eat. I see my phone in a basket on the table. I want to grab it, but I know my mother will get suspicious if I ask for it before breakfast. Dad sips a cup of coffee and looks through a stack of papers.

"You're still not dressed?"

"She's not feeling one hundred percent," says my mother.

"Well, too bad I'm a dentist and not a medical doctor, or I might be able to give you a shot to help you feel better lickety-split," my father says with a grin.

"No, Daddy!"

"She's lying, so she should get her shot in the behind." Cole tries to whack me with a dish towel.

"Am not! You just want to stay here with me and Mom." I scoot my bottom out of his way and then sit down and put my head in my hands.

"Sophie really does seem sick." My mother turns to Dad. "Can you drive Cole to school, Honey? I think I'll keep her home."

"Okay, come on, Champ." Dad takes one last sip from his cup. "Get your backpack. Let's stop off for some donuts on the way in."

"Yay, donuts!" Cole pumps his fist in the air. "Bye, Mom." He kisses her cheek.

My mouth waters. I wish I could get donuts too. I guess I'll have to settle for a bowl of the oatmeal my mother has just put on the stove. I can't believe I'm getting away with this so easily, but I usually rush to get to school to see my friends, so my mother doesn't suspect anything.

"After you eat, why don't you lie down?" She places an aspirin in my hand. "And take this with some water."

I pretend to chew the medicine and slip it in the napkin beside me.

My mother calls the school to let them know I won't be in today.

"Can I pick up her missed work when I get my son later today? Great. Thank you."

"I'm going to go take a shower. Just rest here, and I'll be back in a few minutes," says Mom.

"Alright," I answer. Once she's out of the room, I rush over to the basket to check my cell phone. It wasn't charged last night, so I'm glad the battery is not dead.

There's no message from Chloe. When I look online the crazy picture of me is still there. There aren't any new likes and comments, so people must be looking at something else. But still. Chloe didn't answer me.

Chapter 6

Day Off

Besides my worries about Chloe, I have a nice day off from school. In the morning, Mom lets me watch an old movie from the couch, and Bertram snuggles on the floor near my feet. I love hanging out in our family room, because it's super comfy. There are plenty of soft pillows on the brown leather couch and framed pictures of our family on the walls. I eat a lunch of chicken noodle soup and crackers from a TV tray, and then I catch up on my schoolwork. My teachers emailed work, and I have extra copies of most of my books here at home to use for my assignments.

First, I do some math problems, and then I begin my English paper. When we started learning about poetry, most of the kids in my class complained.

"Why can't poets just say what they mean instead of writing in riddles?" asked Toby. "Half this stuff doesn't make sense to me."

"Roses are red, violets are blue. I think poetry is the pits. How about you?" said Carlton.

I like figuring out what the words in a poem really mean. It's like being a detective.

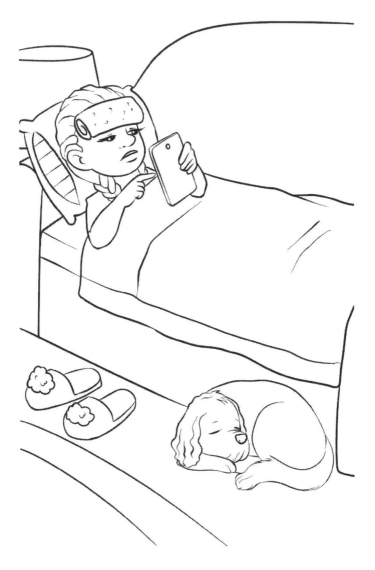

We're studying a poem called *Dreams* by Langston Hughes, an African American writer who died in the 1900s. I read through it:

Hold fast to dreams
For if dreams die
Life is a broken-winged bird
That cannot fly.
Hold fast to dreams
For when dreams go
Life is a barren field
Frozen with snow.

I think I get it. Life is not as great as it can be if you don't have dreams. Interesting. The word "barren" is new to me so I look it up. Lonely, empty, and deserted, says the online dictionary. *If you don't follow your dreams, your life won't be as great as it could be, and you will be lonely and sad,* I write.

I look up some more poems by Langston Hughes. One on friendship gets my attention.

"*I loved my friend*
He went away from me
There's nothing more to say
The poem ends,
Soft as it began-
I loved my friend."

I hope this isn't what happens with me and Chloe. We were best buddies until yesterday, and now it seems like we're drifting apart. If she stops being friends with me, who will I talk to about my favorite TV shows, or shop at the mall with, or look up to? She's the best friend ever and I sure don't want to lose her.

"How is our little home schooler feeling this evening?" says Dad, when he and Cole stroll in from the garage around four o'clock.

"Much better, Daddy," I say. "What are you doing home so early?"

"I had a root canal and some wisdom teeth to pull this morning, and then took an early afternoon to pick up your brother," he says.

"Yeah, we got slushes on the way home," says Cole, sticking out a tongue dyed blue from the raspberry flavored drink. "and this morning I had a bag full of donut holes that I didn't have to share. Yum!"

"Don't you think you're going a bit overboard?" my mother looks at my father and shakes her head. "Next thing you know I'll have another child home with an upset stomach."

"Sorry, Honey, you're right," says Dad, giving her a side hug. "I got a little carried away. It's not every day that I get to take my little man to and from school. Come on, Champ, let's shoot some hoops before you settle down to your homework so we can work off some of that slushy."

"Yay!" Cole cheers.

My mother moves to the kitchen to start dinner. While she was home with me, she spent most of the day finishing up paperwork for her job at my Dad's office.

"How about baked chicken tonight? I downloaded a recipe with a special sauce I think you all will like."

"Sounds good, Mom. Can I have my phone back?" I say. "I want to ask my friends if anything happened at school today."

"Here you go." She reaches in the basket filled with electronics and hands it to me. "I still expect this to be turned in this evening. No phones in your room at bedtime."

"Yes, Ma'am." I press the on button and quickly scroll to the text area. There are "Get Well" messages from Valentina, Mariama, and even Toby, but nothing from Chloe. This is so strange. Is something wrong with her? We always check on each other when one of us is sick. I tap Chloe's phone number and hug my pillow to my chest.

"Hey, bestie!" I say when she answers on the first ring.

"Oh hi, Sophie," she says. "What's up?"

"I didn't come to school today, because I got sick after Pleasure Pier and felt funny this morning."

"Oh yeah, somebody said something about that at lunch." Paper rustles in the background. "Toby and Nathan wanted me to see if you could help them with poetry when you come back to school. You okay now?"

"Yeah, I feel better," I say. "Sure, I can help. I worked on mine today. Hey, Chloe, did you get that text I sent you about the picture you copied?"

"Uh-huh," she says.

"When I looked online a few minutes ago, it was still there."

"Seriously, Sophie, you can be so *extra* sometimes! What's the big deal?" says Chloe. "I was going to delete it. I just got busy."

"Well, can you do it now?"

"Whatever."

"Why are you acting so funny?"

"Why are *you* being so sensitive?" says Chloe. "You're such a Smarty Pants that you can't even take a joke."

"It wasn't funny to me, Chloe. It hurt my feelings. The whole class was laughing at that picture."

"Fine, I'll take it down."

There is an awkward silence.

"I guess I'll see you tomorrow at school," I say.

"Yeah, see you," answers Chloe. "Bye."

"Bye, Chloe."

We both click off our phones, and I bite my lip. I should be happy that Chloe agreed to take down the picture. But why do I feel so bad?

Chapter 7

Chill Out

My heart beats as fast as a hamster runs on a wheel when I walk toward my locker the next morning. Chloe and the rest of our crew usually gather there before classes. Will she even talk to me? After our phone conversation yesterday, I wonder if I still have a best friend.

"Hey, Sophie!" Mariama says as I approach the four kids dressed in our required Xavier Academy school uniforms of khaki skirts and pants and red polo shirts. Chloe, who has jazzed her outfit up with a big, red hair bow, has her back to me and is searching through her locker, so I can't see her face.

"Hi everybody," I say. My nerves settle down as I move in closer to the other kids.

Even though I've known Chloe the longest and she's my BFF, I love all my friends. Mariama and Valentina are on the cheerleading team with Chloe and me, and are loads of fun at sleepovers and just hanging out. I like talking to the boys in our group too, and I used to have a crush on Toby. Chloe also likes Toby, but she won't admit it.

"We missed you at school yesterday," says Valentina. "Hope you feel better." She looks in the pink framed mirror that hangs in her locker with a magnet and runs a comb through her long, straight, black hair before closing it.

"I was able to do a lot of my work at home yesterday, so I don't have anything to make up," I say.

"Well, we know how serious the precious school work is to 'Little Miss Straight A,'" says Chloe, who turns around and slams her metal locker door shut. "Wouldn't want to miss not one assignment now would we, Sophie?"

"Wow, that was harsh, Chlo," says Valentina. "If I missed a day of school, I'd be happy that I wasn't behind in my work either."

"Yeah, these teachers at Xavier don't play when it comes to piling on the homework," says Toby, joining the conversation. "Speaking of which, did Chloe remind you that I need to ask you some questions about that poetry assignment? Can I show you what I have at free period today? It's due on Friday."

"Sure, Toby," I say. "but only if you can look over mine too."

Chloe smacks her lips. "As if yours won't be just what the teacher wants, Sophie."

"Awesome!" says Toby, flashing his deep dimples. "How about meeting in the library?"

"Okay," I say. "See you there."

"Hey, Nathan, you guys going to shoot some hoops in the gym before class starts?" Toby waves goodbye to us and follows a group of boys from our grade down the crowded hallway.

Once he's out of sight, Chloe picks up her sparkly red backpack, also ready to leave. "See you guys later. I've got to get to class early."

"Hey, wait, I was going that way too," I say, bending over to get my things, but she's already gone.

"Dang, she's sure been acting like Cruella de Vil, lately," says Valentina. "Why's she so crabby? Maybe Princess Chloe is jealous that someone else is getting attention from Toby." She looks at me and winks.

"Chloe's in trouble in English," says Mariama, who is in a lot of classes with her. "She met with Mr. Bartee yesterday to go over her paper."

"She needs to chill out," says Valentina. "Chloe gets too mad when everything isn't going her way."

"Maybe you guys should ask her if she wants to work on poetry with you during free period too," suggests Mariama.

"Maybe," I say. "But I don't want her to think that I'm acting like she's not smart enough to do it herself."

"I'd help, but you know that I don't always get As in English," says Valentina.

"Let's get a study group together for everybody," says Mariama. "That way, anyone who needs help can ask questions without being embarrassed."

"Okay, good idea," I say, as the final warning bell rings. "You tell Chloe. We better get to homeroom before we're late. See you all later."

Chapter 8

Free Period

Chloe agrees to meet us in free period, and I feel like someone took a ton of heavy bricks out of my backpack. Once she sees that I'm on her side, maybe she'll stop acting so weird about people coming to me for help with their schoolwork and we can go back to being best friends.

I love Xavier's library. It smells like cupcakes since our librarian, Mrs. Granger, sometimes lights scented candles at her desk. Posters with scenes from the latest books are hung on the wall. Cozy orange and yellow bean bags are scattered amongst the tables and chairs. During free period, kids pack in the library to read books, do homework, and play board games. I sit down at a free table near the entrance and wait for my friends.

"Alright, let's get this party started!" Toby joins me.

"Have you started on your paper at all, Toby?" I say.

"Yes, here's what I have so far." He pushes his black and white marbled notebook toward me.

"Here, you go over mine." I pass my paper to him before I begin reading.

"This is good," I say, looking over his work. "I don't know why you asked for my help."

"Thanks, Sophie," he says. "I thought it sounded okay, but sometimes I don't get what Mr. Bartee wants on these things. Math and science are so much easier for me, you know? There's just one answer; one plus one equals two."

"I hear you," I say. "but as long as what you write explains the poem you can't go wrong."

"That's what you did on your paper." He passes it back to me.

"I see Miss Smarty Pants is already working." Chloe and Mariama approach our table. She slides into a seat as smoothly as a ballerina and then pulls out a floral-print binder from her bag.

"Let's see what our 'class genius' has on her paper." Chloe picks up my sheet and starts reading what I wrote out loud. "'*If you don't follow your dreams, your life won't be as great as it could be and you will be lonely and sad.*' This doesn't make sense. The poem talks about birds with broken wings. It doesn't say anything about life being great, or sad people."

"That's the whole point of poems," I say. "To use words to show feelings and ideas. Finding the meanings of poems seems hard until you get the hang of it, but to me, it's kind of fun."

Chloe reads more of my paper and writes something down in her binder.

"I didn't really understand poetry, but now that I've been talking to you, Sophie, it is more interesting," says Toby, reading the poem from his book again.

"Well, I think studying poetry is stupid." Chloe slides my paper across the table and stands up, "and any-one who likes this stuff is dumb too. Why do we need

English class when we can already speak English? Come on Mariama, this is a waste of time. Let's go to the gym for the rest of free period. I want to work on my front walkover for cheer."

"Chloe, wait!" I say.

"We don't want to take up your precious study time with Toby, Sophie," says Chloe. "Anyway, I've already finished my paper. I don't need your help."

Mariama looks torn, but walks off with Chloe.

I sniff to keep from crying as Toby stuffs his notebook and pencil into his book bag. "I don't know what her deal is," he says. "Your paper is great, Sophie. Thanks for reading mine. Now that you've explained poetry to me, I think I can work on this some more tonight to get a better grade."

"Thanks, Toby. I hope it helps." I wipe the corner of my eye.

The dismissal bell rings, and we walk out of the library.

"Gotta get my other notebook out of my locker," says Toby. "See you later."

I nod and head to the car pool line for pick-up. I feel like I got a bad test grade and stepped in Bertram's dog poo, all rolled into one. Hopefully whatever is bothering Chloe will blow over in the next few days and we can be friends again.

Chapter 9

Left Out

I thought about texting or calling Chloe last night, but decided not to. She didn't call me either. Once I see her again, I hope I can explain that I didn't mean to make her feel bad about the poetry, and we can get back to being best friends.

Cole can't find his reading log, so I get to school later than usual in the morning. By the time I arrive at our lockers, Mariama and Chloe are moving down the hall to homeroom. I feel funny calling out to them like I normally would, so I don't say anything.

At lunchtime, Chloe, Valentina, and Mariama sit way at the end of the rectangular table from me, so we can't talk. I don't worry about it because Toby and Nathan have me laughing with their descriptions of what went on in computer class.

"Mr. Perrier passed gas, and then tried to play it off like the chair moved!" says Nathan.

"It smelled so bad that the janitor asked if somebody got sick when he came in to empty the trash cans!" Toby pinched his nose.

"I wonder what that dude ate for breakfast?" says Nathan. "I couldn't wait to get out of there when the bell rang!"

"You guys are gross!" I push my turkey sandwich to the side.

"Hey, are you all signing up to pay for free dress day?" Toby points to a sign on the cafeteria wall that says we can pay $5 next Friday to dress out of uniform.

"Nah. My dad says it's just a grab for money," says Nathan. "You?"

"I might, to have a break from wearing a uniform," says Toby, who always dresses in the latest sports gear when we're out of school.

"What about you, Sophie?"

I look down at the other end of the table. Sometimes my friends and I wear matching outfits on free dress days, but they haven't heard our conversation and are clearing their things off the table to leave.

"I'm not sure," I say.

I don't see Chloe, Mariama and Valentina in the halls the rest of the school day. But in the afterschool pick-up line, they all hop into her mom's SUV with sleeping and duffle bags. They're having a sleepover and didn't invite me!

I hide myself in the crowd to keep from being noticed. If they see me watching, I'd be totally embarrassed.

"Mom's over there!" Cole calls from the lower school line. I trudge over to him, and we both slide into our car. As we drive away from the school grounds, it starts to sprinkle, and I slouch down in my seat.

Chapter 10

Invitation

"How was school today, kids?" asks my mother. "Are you excited about this weekend?"

A new superhero movie just came out, and this morning my father said he was taking us to Hollywood Cinemas to see it. It's the nicest movie theater in our area and has movie screens so big you can see the tiniest blade of grass even from the back row. I love the comfy seats that lean all the way back. You don't have to go to the concession stand to order your food; just push a button and the server comes to your seat. They have the best popcorn, and sometimes Mom and Dad let us order movie candy too.

"Can I wear my Black Panther costume, Mom?" says Cole. "Wakanda forever!"

"Sure, that's fine. Would you guys like to bring any friends to the movie with us?" says Mom. "What about Jake from down the street, Cole? We can scoop him up on our way to the cinema."

My little brother nods his head with excitement. "Yay! Jake is nice."

"Which of your friends do you want to invite,

Sophie?" says Mom. "I know it may be hard to choose since there are so many girls you hang out with, but you can only bring one. Dad's SUV seats just six people."

I stare out the window and don't answer.

"Did you hear me talking to you?" says Mom.

"I don't want to invite anyone," I say.

"If she's not bringing anybody can I invite Rhythm and Blu?" asks Cole. "They're my size, so we should all fit."

"I'm surprised that you don't want to bring any of your friends, Sophie," says my mother, glancing in the rearview mirror. "You girls do everything together."

"I don't have any friends!" I choke back a sob.

"That's not true, Sophie," says Mom. "You have plenty of friends. What about Chloe, Mariama, and Valentina?"

"They don't like me anymore," I say with a sniffle.

"Just this week I heard you talking on the phone with those girls," says my mother. "Why would they suddenly not like you?"

"I, I, don't know," I say through my tears. "but I saw them bringing their stuff to school for a sleepover, and they didn't invite me."

"That doesn't make sense," says Mom. "There must be some misunderstanding."

"I understand it," says Cole. "Sophie's a Meanie. No wonder they don't want her around."

"Be quiet, Cole!" I sob. "You're the one who's mean!"

"Cole, that's enough," says Mom in a warning tone. She reaches a tissue back to me as we stop at a stop light. "How long have you felt this way, Sophie?"

"Ever since we went to Pleasure Pier and Toby asked me to help with his poetry homework, Chloe's been mad at me," I say and wipe my runny nose with the tissue. "She said my poetry paper was stupid and that I was stupid for liking poems, and now she's turned Valentina and Mariama against me!"

The entrance sign to my neighborhood whizzes by in a blur through my tears.

"Now, sweetie, try not to be so upset," says my mother. "The other girls may not realize what's going on. You were out of school sick earlier this week, so it's not strange that you wouldn't be allowed to go to a sleepover. I'm sure they are still your friends."

"Well then why is Chloe not talking to me?!" I say. "I didn't do anything to her, and now she doesn't want to be my friend anymore."

"I'm sorry this is happening, dear," says my mother as we pull into the driveway. She pushes the garage door opener. "Chloe may be a little jealous. She struggles with her dyslexia, and though we know how hard you study, it may seem to her like things come easier to you. Give it time, and things may settle down."

"What am I going to do until then?" I cry. "My friends are all having fun this weekend, and I'm doing nothing."

"Yes, you are. You're going to the movie with us!" says Cole. "and that will be way better than staying up giggling with some icky girls."

"Your sister may not feel that way, Cole" says Mom with a chuckle. "but your brother does have a point. Friends come and go, but your family will always be here for you. I know things seem bad now, but I can almost guarantee that you'll feel better soon. Try to have fun this weekend. Invite another friend to come to the movie with us."

While Mom makes a call to Jake's parents and Cole rolls around the family room floor with Bertram, I think about what she just said. Chloe and the other girls are probably getting an afterschool snack, laughing, and planning what movies they'll stay up watching, while I'm crying. Maybe if I did bring another friend to the movies with us, things wouldn't feel so bad.

"Can I invite Rani?" I ask when Mom joins me in the kitchen.

"She was on your computer coding team, right?" she says. "That's a great idea."

The rain has stopped falling and the sun peeks out from the clouds. Maybe this weekend won't be as bad after all.

Chapter 11

Hollywood Cinemas

I feel like a track runner crossing the finish line the next morning after I find out Rani can go to the movies with us. I bounce into my bunny slippers and prance to my dresser to shake a couple of flakes of fish food into Goldy's bowl before I join my family downstairs.

My heart skips a beat when I see a photo booth printout of me and Chloe under a hair tie on my dresser. It's from her birthday last year. We have white feather boas around our necks and are grinning like the Cheshire Cat from *Alice in Wonderland*. I wonder if I'll ever have such good times with my BFF again.

I shake my head to get my friend problems off my mind as I walk downstairs. This is going to be a great day!

Dad is even more excited than Cole to see the superhero movie.

"This is the final episode in the trilogy," he says, and scrolls through a movie trailer on his phone. "I've been waiting all year to find out how everything turns out."

"Me too!" says Cole, bouncing up and down.

I hope I'll be able to follow what is going on. I'm not really into superheroes and haven't seen the first two movies in the series.

Cole is dressed in his Black Panther costume, and his friend Jake has a Captain America suit on.

"I hope nobody I know sees us," I say with a cringe.

"You boys look adorable," says my mother, patting Cole on the head. "I love your costume, Jake."

"Thank you for inviting me to the movie, Mrs. Washington," says Jake.

Jake is eight years old like Cole, but he goes to the elementary school in our neighborhood, so they've never been in the same class. They get along great and play outside together all the time. Cole's other good friends on our block are Rhythm and Blu, whose parents gave them such funny names because their dad is a jazz musician.

Cole and Jake get in the back row of Dad's SUV, and I check the middle row carefully before sitting down because Cole loves to put whoopee cushions and other things in my seat to prank me.

"Yay! There's Rani," Cole says when we pull up to her driveway. Cole thinks most of my friends are boring or "icky," but he likes Rani because she tells silly jokes just like he does.

"Hi, Sophie! Hi Mr. and Mrs. Washington!" Rani's long black ponytail bounces as she bounds from her front door to meet us. Her parents wave goodbye from the front porch.

"Glad you could join us, Rani," says Dad.

"I can't wait to see this movie!" Rani slides in beside me. "The previews look awesome."

"You like super hero movies?" I widen my eyes.

"Yeah, doesn't everybody?"

"Spoken like my kind of girl!" says Dad.

"Hey, Rani, I have a joke for you," says Cole. "What did Superman say to Spider Man?"

"I don't know, what?" she turns her head towards the back row.

"Don't bug me!"

"That's a good one," says Rani. "Listen to this joke. What did they call T'Challa when he was a baby? Black Pampers!"

Cole and Jake fall out laughing, and Mom and Dad giggle too.

"What minute, who's T'Challa?" I say.

"The hero of the movie we're going to see, and the person whose costume I'm wearing," says Cole.

"Yeah, you don't know that?" says Jake.

"You've got a lot of info to catch up on, Sophie," says Rani. She notices that I look embarrassed. "But don't worry, I'll answer any questions you have at the movie."

On the way to Hollywood Cinemas, Rani tells us what she's been up to. "My Indian dance teacher is taking us to a competition in Dallas," she says, "so we practice for two hours on Saturday mornings. I usually have academic team practice on Saturday afternoons, but they gave us the day off today."

"You certainly are a busy young lady," says my mother. "I'm glad you were able to come with us."

"Me too," says Rani. "Sophie and I aren't around each other a lot at school, so it's good to see her."

I'm glad I listened to my Mom and brother and brought along a friend, because Rani and I are having a great time talking about our classes at Xavier and joking around with Cole and Jake.

"Maybe you can come watch my dance team perform sometime," says Rani.

"Sounds like fun."

The line at the cinema seems about a mile long, but luckily, my Dad bought our tickets online before we left home. Giant black and white pictures with old-time movie stars on them hang on the dark walls. There is a red carpet that snakes to the front entrance like they have in Hollywood. We're able to move to the front when the cashier waves us into the theater. Other people in the crowd are dressed in costumes like Cole and Jake, so they don't look too weird.

We move to Section B, to find our assigned seats, and someone calls out to us from our row.

"Hey, Sophie, aren't those your boyfriends from school?" Cole points to the left. I squint my eyes in the dim lighting to get a better view.

It's Toby and Nathan!

Chapter 12

New Friends

"Your sister is too young to have a boyfriend." My father turns to me and frowns.

"No, Dad, they are just friends from my school."

"Hey, Sophie and Rani, I didn't know you guys were into super hero movies," says Toby. Nathan waves from the seat beside him, and I wave back.

"Want to sit next to your boyfriends so you can get some smooches before the movie starts?" says Cole. He elbows Jake and they both start laughing.

"Be quiet, Cole!" I say under my breath.

"Let's sit down so we don't disturb anyone," whispers Dad. He and my mother take our assigned seats by the aisle, and Cole and Jake are next to them, so Rani and I end up beside Toby and Nathan.

As my eyes adjust to the dimmed lighting, I glance around the theater. There are twenty rows of cushiony red leather chairs behind the movie screen that's as wide as about three big beds. Our row is in the middle of the theater, giving us a great view. I plop in my chair and lean it back so that my sneakers rise up in the air on the foot rest. If I don't like the movie, I can take a nice nap.

The theater is packed, and filled with sounds of forks clinking on plates and people whispering food orders. My mouth waters when I catch a whiff of some nachos and candy in the row in front of us.

"Let's get some popcorn!" says Rani, pushing the button for the server.

"The snacks in here are the best," says Toby crunching on a French fry.

"Yeah, I live for the wings," says Nathan.

"You guys came by yourselves?" I ask.

"Nah, I stayed over Nathan's house last night and his mom is taking his little cousin to some movie about a dancing school in the other theater. We got our tickets at the last minute. His dad is a couple rows back from us."

"I've been waiting to see this movie for months," says Rani.

I'm tongue tied. Though I'm happy to see the boys, I know that Chloe will be mad if she finds out we sat next to them. I think it was mean of her not to invite me to her sleepover, but deep down I'm still hoping we can make up once we go back to school on Monday.

"I'm surprised you don't have Chloe and the rest of your crew with you," says Toby. "What are they doing this weekend?"

"If she's smart, she'll be studying for English," says Nathan. "I heard her talking to Mr. Bartee after class the other day, and she didn't look too happy."

"Yeah, that class is hard," says Toby. "Thanks for going over my paper with me, Sophie. I think I should get a pretty good grade."

"Sophie is the best at English," says Rani.

I smile and blush.

The previews start, and the lights go down. Our server brings Rani and me a big tub of popcorn to share, and Mom and Dad let us order slushes too. Cole and Jake get chicken wings, and thankfully he doesn't spill or drop anything.

I end up liking the movie, though there are some parts I don't understand since I haven't seen the other movies in the series. Toby and Nathan barely make a sound the entire time the movie is on. They are really into this stuff.

"That was incredible!" says Toby, when the final scene ends.

"It was way better than I thought it would be," I agree.

"My favorite part was when the Cyborgs returned to their planet," says Rani.

"I know, I wasn't expecting that," says Nathan.

"Wakanda forever!" says Cole, pumping his fist in the air.

"Now I want to see some of the older movies," I say, as we walk up the aisle to the cinema lobby.

"This one was the best, but the others are great too," says Toby. I squint as my eyes get used to the bright light. Nathan walks over with his father and they scan the crowd to find his mother and cousin.

As we've been talking to the boys, Cole and Jake stand behind them puckering their lips and making kissing sounds. I want to smack my brother. Thank goodness the crowd is so loud that Toby and Nathan don't notice.

"Anybody need a restroom break before we head out?" says my father walking behind my brother and Jake.

"I do," says my mother. "I drank a tall glass of water, plus a soda, but the movie was so good I didn't want to leave."

"I read online that some people planned on wearing pull ups to this movie so they wouldn't have to miss anything," says Dad.

"I can totally see somebody doing that!" says Nathan with a laugh.

"Eww, I wonder if anybody did that in here?" says Cole. "Diapers forever!"

Everybody cracks up. I want to hide.

"Your little brother is so funny, Sophie!" says Rani.

More like, so embarrassing. I am grateful when Nathan sees his cousin's blond hair, and the conversation ends.

"Let's head out, fellas." Nathan's father motions for the boys to follow them.

"See you at school on Monday, Sophie," says Toby.

"See you."

Chapter 13

Green Eyed Monster

"Hey, Sophie, your shirt is on inside out!" Valentina calls out to me as I hook my bright, yellow jacket in my locker. I put my hand by my neck and feel the tag on the outside of my polo.

The warning bell rings for homeroom, and Chloe and Marima put their hands over their mouths to hide their giggles.

Can anything worse happen today? Dad was mad at me and Cole this morning because, while we were arguing about whose turn it was to empty the dishwasher, Bertram sneaked out to the shoe rack in the garage and chewed up one of his favorite loafers. Then at breakfast, Cole dropped his bowl of cereal with milk in it on the floor and my mother made me help him clean it up.

Since I've been at school, my three best friends have barely spoken to me, and now they are laughing about my clothes.

"Oh no!" I say. "I don't have time to fix it before class, and we aren't allowed to wear any jackets that aren't part of our school uniform."

"'No problemo," says Valentina. She throws her school cardigan to me. "Put this on. You can change once you get out of class."

"Thanks, Valentina," I say with a smile. She gives me the thumbs up sign.

"You'd think you would be able to put your clothes on the right way, as smart as everyone says you are, Sophie," says Chloe with a smirk.

I put my arms through the sleeves on Valentina's sweater and don't say anything.

"Hi guys." Toby strolls up to us and smiles.

"Hey, Toby. How was your weekend?" says Chloe.

"Pretty good. Did you all see that new superhero movie? It was off the chain, wasn't it, Sophie?"

"Yeah, my Dad says we're going to rent one of the other ones for movie night, next week, so I'll be caught up."

"Sweet. Let me know what you think," says Toby.

Chloe frowns. "You guys went to the movies together?"

"Our seats were by each other at the cinema," says Toby. "I had never hung out with Rani before. She's really cool."

"Yeah, she is nice," I say.

"Chloe said your parents don't let you go anywhere with friends if you miss school," says Mariama. "We thought you had to stay home, or we would have invited you to our sleepover."

"That's usually true," I say, "but I was feeling okay, and my father had pre-ordered tickets to the movie."

"My little brother Hector loves super heroes and wants us to take him, but my grandma says he's too little since it's PG-13," says Valentina. "I really want to see *Dance Off.*"

"Maybe we can go see it this weekend," says Chloe.

"Can you come too, Sophie?" asks Mariama.

"She probably has studying to do," says Chloe.

Mariama and Valentina look confused.

"I can get my homework done early," I say.

"We'll see," says Chloe. "Come on, Mariama, we better get going if we don't want to be late to homeroom."

"See you, Sophie." Mariama looks over her shoulder.

"See you," I say.

Chloe doesn't even answer. I can tell my friends realize something is up between us. I am getting tired of all the drama but I don't know what to say to Chloe. This can't go on forever. I've got to get up my nerve to talk to her about it.

Chapter 14

Plagi-What?

"Sophie, can I see you after class?"

Mr. Bartee, our English teacher, says right before the bell rings.

"Uh, oh, somebody's in trouble," whispers Nathan from the desk to my right.

I squirm in my seat. I wonder why the teacher is calling me out? I get straight A's in his class. We turned in our poetry papers on Friday afternoon. Maybe mine wasn't as good as I thought it was, and he's giving me a chance to redo it.

I twirl my purple, sparkly pencil in my hand until class is over, and the other students file out. I'm annoyed because the next class is a free period and I was planning on finishing up some of my homework.

I glance nervously at the open door and hope that none of my other classmates see that I'm in a meeting with the teacher. When Mr. Bartee walks to my side I stiffen.

"Thanks for staying, Sophie," he says. "This won't take long. Your poetry essay was excellent. But when I graded a few other papers I found one that used the exact words as yours on a couple of sentences. Do you know what plagiarism is? We talked about it before we started writing our papers."

Plagi-what? My stomach drops like I'm going down a hill on the Killer Whale.

"That's cheating, right?" I say, remembering the lesson we had at the beginning of our poetry unit. "Plagiarism is copying someone else's ideas or words and using them as your own."

"Exactly. The other student I spoke with says that they wrote their paper independently. I wanted to check with you to get your side before moving forward."

My chest tightens, and I begin to get mad.

"I didn't copy anyone's paper, Mr. Bartee," I say. "I started working on mine on Tuesday when I was home from school."

"You're one of my best students," says Mr. Bartee. "I just need to check out the situation, since the other student in question also says that they did their work themselves."

"Who is it? How could someone copy my paper? I had it in my English binder until I turned it in."

There's a light knock on the doorway. I stop talking and turn to look as a shadow fills the doorway.

It's Chloe!

"Hi, Mr. Bartee. Umm, my teacher told me you wanted to see me again?" she says.

"Oh, yes, Chloe. Come in," he waves her to the empty desk beside me. "I asked Sophie about her poetry paper, and she says she wrote it herself. Are you sure that this is your work?" He holds up a paper with a bright red A+ on it, and Chloe sits up taller.

"Yes, sir. That's my work. I wrote it myself, but Sophie and I studied together in free period the other day. Maybe she copied my notes by mistake and thought they were hers. Remember, Sophie, you asked to look at my paper since you said you were still finishing yours?"

"Is this true, Sophie?"

I look at Chloe and she nods.

"I..I..guess so," I rub my hand on my lap.

"So, it's possible that you remembered words you saw on Chloe's paper when you were completing yours?"

I bite my lip and silently start counting down from ten.

My English teacher shakes his head. "I thought it was a bit unusual that you seem to get As on every assignment, Sophie, but I never thought you might cheat. Chloe's been coming to me for help with the paper every day since I assigned it, so I know she's been working hard."

"But…" I begin, and Chloe kicks my foot. "I mean, I didn't think it was cheating. I just looked at Chloe's notes for ideas."

"So, you're saying you used some of the same words from her notes on your paper?" he asks.

Chloe widens her eyes and I nod my head up and down. Even though it's not the truth, I don't want to get her in trouble. Then she'll be even madder at me.

"Yes, I copied Chloe's notes."

"This is serious," Mr. Bartee says. "It's good that we are dealing with this early so that you won't think it's okay later. You'll be writing many papers throughout middle and high school, and it's best to nip bad habits in the bud now. I'm sorry, but I'm going to have to reduce your grade 50 points, Sophie." He makes a mark on my paper with his bright red pen, and writes something down in his grade book. "I saw the sentences that were on both your papers on Chloe's notes when she came to me with a question on Thursday, so I figured it was her work, but I had to make sure. It's best to work on papers by yourself and not in groups."

"Yes, sir," says Chole.

"Yes, Mr. Bartee." I sniff back tears.

"Your average is so high already, Sophie, that this shouldn't lower your grade in the class too much," says our teacher. "but I hope you've learned a lesson. You ladies are dismissed."

It's warm in the room, but I feel like I'm outside on a cold day. I rub the goosebumps on my arms and squint to keep from crying, and then I pick up my backpack and follow Chloe.

"Whew, that was close," she says after we shut the door. "Thanks for having my back in there, bestie."

I don't answer. Chloe doesn't notice how upset I am.

"Now that I got an A on that poetry paper, I may make the honor roll for the first time." She grins wider than a smiling emoji. "I can't wait to tell my parents!"

"Mr. Bartee thinks I cheated," I say, still shaken.

"It's no biggie," says Chloe. "He knows you're smart, and the points he's taking off won't even change your grade in the class. Hey, I gotta go to see my tutor, but Mariama and Valentina are coming over to my house to make tie-dye shirts after school. You want to come?"

I shrug my shoulders. "All right."

"Okay, see you at lunch!" Chloe practically skips down the hallway, while I walk to my locker like I'm trudging through ankle deep mud.

Toby bounces up as I drift through the crowd of kids in the hallway. "Everything okay, Soph?" Nathan told me Mr. Bartee had you stay after in English class. What did he want?"

"Nothing really," I say. "He just wanted to talk to me and Chloe about our poetry papers."

"Man, am I happy we're done with that unit!" says Toby. "I feel lucky I got a B. Mr. Bartee ask you to tutor Chloe or something? Your paper was the bomb."

"I wish." My stomach flutters like it's filled with butterflies, and then I hit my palm on my head. "Oops, I forgot something in my locker! I need to go back to get it. See you later, Toby."

"Oh, okay, see you." He watches in confusion as I rush the other way down the hall.

The last thing I want to talk about is my English paper, or Chloe. She's not mad anymore, and I should be happy, shouldn't I? Even though I got in trouble with Mr. Bartee, I have As on all my English assignments, so having points off the poetry paper probably won't change my report card grade. If I do really well on my other work, Mom and Dad won't ever have to find out about this.

Chloe invited me to hang out with her, Mariama, and Valentina after school, which means things are back to normal with us. So why do I feel like I've lost my best friend all over again?

Chapter 15

Tie Dye

At the end of the school day I text Mom about Chloe's invitation, and she's excited.

I knew you girls would make up! Chloe's mother has already called me. I have a meeting this afternoon, so Mariama's parents can drop you home.

Mariama and Valentina are glad to see me as we wait for Chloe in the car pool area.

"You're coming too, Sophie?!" says Valentina. "Fantastico!"

"This is going to be so much fun!" says Mariama. "I love doing tie-dye!"

"I'm going to take lots of pictures of the shirts we make," says Valentina. "Maybe we can wear them to free dress day on Friday."

"Great idea!" says Mariama. "I want mine to be really colorful."

"Hey, guys! Ready to leave?" Chloe interrupts the conversation. "Let's go! My mom is over there. Come on, Sophie!"

She wraps her arm around my shoulder as we walk across the parking lot.

"Hello girls! How was your day today?" Mrs. Hopkins, who is an older, more glamorous version of Chloe, greets us when we get into her car. "So nice to see you, Sophie! We missed you at the sleepover last weekend."

Mariama and Valentina glance at Chloe, and I chew on my fingernail.

"Yeah, she was sick earlier in the week," Chloe says brightly, and then chatters all the way to her house about the tie-dye shirt kits she and her mom bought at the craft store. "They had a sale, and we bought enough for us each to make our own shirt." she says.

"Awesome!" says Valentina.

As soon as we pull into the garage, we grab our belongings and scramble into the kitchen, excited to begin our project.

The Hopkins's kitchen looks like something out of a magazine, with white cabinets, and a shiny, silver stove and refrigerator. There is a huge bunch of red roses in a vase on the counter and the air is filled with the sweet, flowery scent. We set our backpacks in a side area with cubbies before getting ready for our snack.

"I forgot to ask you, Chloe," says Mrs. Hopkins. "How'd you do on that poetry paper?"

Usually Chloe doesn't like to talk about her grades when we're around. I tug at my shirt collar, Valentina pulls out her cell phone, and Mariama picks at her nail polish.

"I got an A!" she says.

"That's wonderful news!" Mrs. Hopkins slaps her hand on the kitchen counter. "I knew all those hours you spent studying would pay off! We need to celebrate! I can't wait to tell your father. I'll heat up a frozen pizza for snack instead of serving the cheese and crackers we planned!"

"Yay!" cheer Valentina and Mariama.

"That's great, Chloe!" says Mariama. "How'd you do it? Mr. Bartee's a really tough grader. I got a B- on mine."

"He loved my writing." She winks at me.

I look down at a crack in the tile floor.

"Let's get started on the tee shirts while the pizza heats up!" says Chloe.

We follow her to the back patio where a giant plastic table cloth is spread on the ground.

"Mom's a real neat freak," says Chloe. "She doesn't want us getting dye everywhere."

Each kit has directions showing you how to twist the tee shirts and wrap rubber bands around them that will make swirling patterns once the shirts are dyed.

"Put these on, everybody, so your hands won't get stained." Chloe passes out rubber gloves along with tubes of dye.

After I slip on the gloves, I choose bright, rainbow colors and squirt them on the folds of fabric.

"The directions say that we have to wrap the shirts in plastic for at least six hours and then wash them," says Mariama. "That means they won't be finished today. I can't wait to see how they turn out!"

"Oooh, look at that purple and pink shirt Chloe is making," says Valentina. "Que bonito!"

"Mom gave me an extra shirt, and I'm making one in the same color for Sophie, so we can be twins," says Chloe with a smile.

I blush. I still feel funny about what happened in English class, but it's nice to be back with my friends.

After we lay our shirt projects on the tablecloth to dry, we head into the kitchen to eat our pizza and start on homework. Every fifteen minutes or so we take a break to laugh and talk. It's like nothing ever went wrong between me and my best friend. Five o'clock rolls around way too soon.

"Mariama and Valentina, your parents are outside for pickup," says Mrs. Hopkins. "Thanks again for coming over to hang out with Chloe. Your shirts should be ready in a couple of days."

"Thank you for having us, Mrs. Hopkins," says Mariama. "It was fun."

"Yeah, thanks!" says Valentina.

"See you guys at school tomorrow," Chloe gives me an extra hug. "Can't wait to wear our tee shirts this Friday, bestie!"

I have a warm feeling as I walk out the door. I have a best friend again.

Chapter 16

Trouble

Mariama's family drops me off, and I use the key pad to get in the garage. I hear sounds of Dad's favorite jazz song in the family room. Good smells come from the kitchen. We'll probably eat dinner early. I'm glad because even though I had a couple of slices of pizza at Chloe's I'm still hungry.

"Sophie's home!" Cole calls as soon as I shut the door.

Bertram jumps up on my leg and barks. I scratch his head, and he starts whining.

"Did you feed him, Cole? It seems like he's starving," I say.

"You're in trou-ble!" Cole singsongs as I set my backpack down, and my stomach drops.

"What are you talking about?"

"Mom got a note from one of your teachers and she and Dad have been fussing about it," he says. "They were going to come get you from Chloe's."

Uh-oh. Mr. Bartee must have emailed them after all.

"Hi, Sophie, how was your day at school?" Dad walks into the kitchen and my mother follows him.

"Uh, it was fine, Dad. Hi Mom."

"Did you have a nice time at Chloe's?" she says.

"Yes, we made lots of tie dye shirts," I speak quickly. "The dye has to stay on them for a while, and then they have to be washed, so they'll be done tomorrow. Chloe made one for me and her to wear as twins on free dress day."

"Sounds good," says Mom.

"We need to talk to you about something in the family room, Sophie," says Dad. "Cole, you sit here and study for your spelling test for a while."

"But I'm already know all my spelling words," he whines.

"Then work on the ones for the next test," says my father.

Cole walks to the kitchen table and slowly opens his spelling book, and I follow my parents. They sit on the couch and Dad pats the empty cushion beside him for me to join them.

"Your English teacher sent us an email this afternoon about something that went on in your class, Sophie," says Mom. "Can you tell us about it?"

I want to shake my head no, but I doubt that will get me out of the pickle I'm in.

"Chloe and I used some of the same words on our poetry paper, so he thought we cheated."

"Mr. Bartee said you admitted to copying Chloe's notes, Sophie, and used them on your paper," says Mom. "Is that true?"

"Well, not exactly..." I answer.

"What do you mean 'not exactly.'" My father raises his voice. "Either you copied off your friend's paper or you didn't."

I wring my hands and don't say anything.

"Does this have anything to do with the fight you girls are having?" says Mom.

"We're not fighting anymore. Chloe and I made up."

"Did you copy her paper?" My father asks again. I sit still as a statue.

"You and Chloe have been friends for a long time," says Mom. "But real friends don't get each other in trouble. Now, I'm not sure what's going on here, but I know that what I read in that email does not sound like the Sophie Washington that we know. I hope we haven't pressured you too much to get good grades. We want you to do well in school, but through honest means."

"Are you going to explain this, Sophie?" says Dad.

I stare at a framed picture of me and Cole on the beach and stay silent.

"Fine. Don't answer us, young lady, but we're not happy about getting messages like this from a teacher," he says. "Hand over your cell phone, and you are grounded until next week. Maybe you should go up to your room for a while to think about what it means to be honest."

"But...."

"We're giving you a chance to clear up what's going on here, but you're not answering us," says Mom. "Just tell us what happened."

I keep quiet.

The disappointed look on my parent's faces makes me want to start crying again. Going along with Chloe seemed like an easy way to get back our friendship, but now that my parents think I cheated too, I'm not sure what to do. If I tell them the truth, they'll tell Mr. Bartee, and Chloe will be mad at me again. It felt so good to be with my friends this afternoon.

I hand Dad my phone and walk slowly up the stairs to my room. Maybe things will make more sense in the morning.

Chapter 17

Book Report

"Sophie, wait!" Chloe rushes up to me as I turn around the corner before first period.

Seeing her is like sunshine on a cloudy day after last night. My parents and I barely spoke at dinner, so Cole went crazy telling all his corny jokes.

"What did the baby corn say to his mom? Where is Pop Corn?"

Mom and Dad smiled, but I know they didn't think the joke was any funnier than I did.

We didn't talk much this morning either, and who knows when my parents will give me my cell phone back.

"Hey, Chloe. What's going on?" I say.

She stands flat footed and faces me directly.

"Mr. Bartee wants me to read my paper in English class." She says in a rush.

"What?! Why?"

"Because it's one of the best ones." She plays with her bracelet.

My stomach churns. I dodge an eighth grader rushing down the hall, and then look Chloe in the eye. "What are you going to do?"

"Read it, I guess. I didn't want you to be surprised if anyone told you."

"I don't know about this, Chloe. I went along with you copying my work and got my grade lowered, but this is too much."

"What's the big deal?" she throws her hands up in the air. "You mad that for once someone else is getting attention besides you?"

"It's not about the attention…"

"You always have to be seen as Miss Smarty Pants, don't you?" Chloe speaks quickly. "It's all about Sophie, the Brainiac. Ever since you won that spelling bee last year, you've thought you were better than me."

"That's not true, and you know it, Chloe. I just don't like people thinking I'm a cheater when I didn't do anything wrong."

"So, you're calling me a cheater, huh?"

"You copied off my paper!" My lips quiver. "How could you do that?!"

"Whatever, Sophie," she holds her hand, palm up, to stop me. "It's your word against mine, and you already admitted to looking at my notes earlier."

She turns on her heels and stomps off down the hall.

I'm so mad I see circles swirling in front of my eyes. I feel like going to Mr. Bartee's room right now to set things straight. But if I tell on Chloe, there's no way we'll stay friends. I guess there's nothing I can do.

Chapter 18

Beyond the Words

My heart sinks to my stomach when I walk into English class and see Chloe standing in the back of the room. She's looking down at a piece of paper that's probably her copy of my essay. All the 6B students are here, along with the rest of the kids from 6A.

"Hey, Sophie! This way!" Mariama waves me to an empty desk beside her, and I slide into the chair. Toby sits behind us.

"Welcome, students!" Mr. Bartee stands in front of the room by the white board. "It's nice to have both of my English classes together. This afternoon you'll have an extra-long P.E. class in the gym while the teachers have training workshops. English is only twenty minutes today, so I decided to do something different and combine both sections to wrap up our unit on poetry."

"Thank goodness," Toby says under his breath.

Mr. Bartee moves to his desk to leave a space in the center of the room. "We finished the unit with our papers on *Dreams,* one of my favorite poems by Langston Hughes. Your essays were very good, but two stood out. I'd like to have both students come up to read their papers."

Toby smiles at me and winks.

"Can Chloe Hopkins and Alexa Gilbert join me up front?"

Toby's eyes widen and he straightens in his chair. Chloe looks ahead as she makes her way to down the aisle with Alexa, a girl with light brown hair and shiny silver braces on her teeth.

"I've asked these two young ladies to read portions of their papers to the class, to give you an idea what I was looking for," says Mr. Bartee. "Alexa, care to go first? Then Chloe can add in a piece from her paper."

"Sure, Mr. Bartee." Alexa smiles with her lips pulled down to cover her braces.

"Dreams are what make life worth living. To enjoy your best life, never let go of your dreams."

Mr. Bartee looks at Chloe and nods.

"If you don't follow your dreams, your life won't be as great as it could be, and you will be lonely and sad." She slowly reads.

Toby's jaw drops.

"Hey, that sounds like your essay!" Mariama whispers.

I bite my lip. I didn't care too much when I let Chloe pretend my paper was hers in Mr. Bartee's room, but now that she's getting credit for my work in front of so many other kids, I feel awful.

"These are excellent examples," says Mr. Bartee. "Both girls looked beyond the words on the paper to find their true meaning."

"Chloe looked beyond the words on her paper to Sophie's," jokes Toby.

"Did you have something to add, Mr. Johnson?" Mr. Bartee turns our way.

Toby raises his eyebrow at me, and I shake my head. "No, sir," Toby says.

"Then let's focus on the ending of the poem," Mr. Bartee continues.

Chapter 19

Speak Up

"Why didn't you say something?" Toby stops me at my locker after class. Nathan and Mariama join us.

"Was that really your paper Chloe was reading?" asks Mariama.

"I…I didn't want to get her in trouble," I say, moving back from them.

"But that's not fair to the rest of us who had to do our papers ourselves," Toby says.

"I got a C on mine," says Nathan. "If I knew you writing people's papers, then I would have met you in the library the other day."

"What's going on, girl?" Chloe sees us arguing and walks up.

"We're asking why you were reading Sophie's paper," says Toby.

"We just shared notes. Sophie was fine with me using it, right, Bestie?" Chloe puts her arm around my shoulder.

I shake my head and move away from her.

"You were my best friend, Chloe," I say, "but you've been so mean to me lately."

"I thought we were cool. Why are you so salty?" Chloe puts her hands on her hips.

"Mr. Bartee emailed my parents, and I got in big trouble, and you don't even care."

"You didn't tell me you got in trouble...." Chloe's cheeks redden.

"It just happened last night. My parents took my cell phone, and now I'm grounded."

"Wow, that's terrible!" says Mariama.

"And you call Sophie your best friend?" says Toby. He shakes his head. "I'll never understand girls. There's no way I'd treat one of my boys like that."

"Yeah, that's messed up," says Nathan.

"We should stay out of this and let Chloe and Sophie talk." Mariama looks back and forth between the two of us.

"Aww man, this was just getting good," says Nathan.

"Come on, Nathan, we need to get to the gym to get changed for P.E.," says Toby, pulling his sleeve.

"See you all later," says Mariama.

They walk off, and Chloe looks down and chews on her bottom lip, not saying anything. Memories of everything that's been going on the past few days wash over me like a water hose on full blast. I can't believe she's not even speaking when I'm in so much trouble.

A burst of energy rushes through me, like when I climb to the top of a cheer pyramid at one of our school basketball games. I pull my shoulders back.

"You know what, Chloe?" I say loudly. "Forget this. You're not my friend, and I never want to talk to you again. I'm done!" I turn my back to her and start turning the combination on my locker with shaking hands.

"Sophie, wait!" She puts her hands on my back and I shrug them off.

"I am your friend," she says. "and I'm sorry."

"Then why have you been acting so crazy the past few days?"

"I dunno…I guess… I was just jealous. My parents have been on my case to raise my grades. They're embarrassed that their daughter is a dummy who never makes the honor roll. I thought using your paper would help me finally get at least a B in English, and that it would be no biggie for you, since your grades are always so high. I didn't mean to get you in trouble."

I slowly turn around. "You're not a dummy, Chloe. I would have helped you with your paper if you'd asked."

"I know. I just get tired of school always being so hard," she says starting to cry. "I study so much, but it never seems to be enough. For once, I wanted to be on the honor roll like all you guys. I hope you won't stay mad at me for being a bad friend."

Chapter 20

BFF

"Is everything okay, over here?" Mr. Bartee walks up to us. Chloe and I are so into our conversation that we didn't notice the warning bell.

"Yes, sir," I say.

"You two need to get to class," he says. "The bell's about to ring. I'll follow you to the gym while I'm on my way to the teacher's workshop."

I shut my locker and grab my backpack. Chloe wipes her eyes with the back of her hand.

"Mr. Bartee," she says with a shaky voice. "I have something to tell you."

I hold my breath as she speaks.

"I didn't tell the truth the other day. I copied notes from Sophie and wrote them on my paper. The essay I read this morning wasn't mine. It was hers."

Mr. Bartee stops a few feet from the door to the school gym and looks at both of us.

"Why would you let Chloe take credit for your work, Sophie?"

I shift my eyes. "Because I wanted to be a good friend."

"Helping someone do the wrong thing isn't being friend to them." He turns to face Chloe. "Nor is taking credit for someone else's work. I've already punished you, Sophie, by reducing your grade and reporting what happened to your parents. I guess I'll have to do the same for you, Chloe."

"Yes, sir," she says with her head down.

He stares at both of us again and shakes his head.

"I need to hurry to the workshop before I'm late. We'll talk more about this incident later. You girls go on to class."

We stand at the doorway before going in to change for P.E. Chattering kids who are already dressed out in their P.E. tee shirts and shorts wander in.

Toby and Carlton and a few other boys start to shoot hoops. Now that the truth is out about my paper, I feel as light as the basketball that swishes through the net.

"I'm sorry you got into trouble with Mr. Bartee, Chloe," I say.

She nervously plays with her bracelet. "I'm sorry I made all this happen in the first place, Sophie. I hope we can be friends again."

"Sure, bestie," I say and put my hand on her shoulder.

Chloe gives me a shy smile and, together, we walk into the girl's locker room.

Chapter 21

Free Dress Day

After I tell my parents the whole story, they're mad.

"I thought you'd have more sense than to do something like that," says Dad.

"You need to stop going along with your friends all the time and start thinking for yourself," says Mom.

Their lectures are annoying, but I know that they are right. If I hadn't let Chloe get away with copying off of me, we might not have gotten into so much trouble. When Mr. Bartee emailed Chloe's parents, they took her phone away too, and I am still on punishment.

My brother is happy I'm grounded, since I'm spending more time with him.

"Want to play Monopoly after dinner?" he asks.

"Again? When am I going to get my phone back, Mom?!"

"When your Dad and I feel like you've learned your lesson," she says. "We'll talk about it next week. In the meantime, it won't hurt you to play some board games with Cole. You were getting too wrapped up in that cell phone anyway."

Though she was also grounded, Chloe's parents let her bring our tie dye shirts to school for free dress day on Friday. The pink and purple ones she made for us to wear as twins are super cute.

"Looks like Chloe and Sophie are back friends again," says Nathan, seeing us in our matching outfits.

"You girls can never stay mad for long, can you?" says Toby with a laugh. "I'm just happy that Sophie stood up for herself for once."

"I guess I can be a bit bossy at times," says Chloe.

"Tell me about it!" says Toby.

Now that we've made up, our friendship is better. I tell Chloe how I really feel about things, and she's stopped being so pushy. I've started hanging out more with other friends too.

It's free period and I sit in the library with Rani. She's making a new video game for our computer coding class, and I'm helping. It's extra crowded today, because Mrs. Granger has brought in a karaoke machine and kids are jumping around to the music.

"Let's make the characters move this way," Rani suggests, clicking the mouse on her computer.

"Good idea," I answer.

"Come on, Sophie, let's get in that dance off with Valentina and Mariama." Chloe comes to over to us and pulls my arm. "I want to show off some of our new cheer moves."

Rani makes a move to pick up her books to leave, but I stop her.

"I can't now, Chloe. I'm busy." I point out our work, and she slows down to look.

"Oh okay, I see you're doing something. Mariama, Valentina, wait up!" She calls over her shoulder as she rushes to join our other friends. "We can hang out later, Sophie."

And I know that we will. That's what friends do.

Dear Reader:

Thank you for reading *Sophie Washington: My BFF*. I hope you liked it. If you enjoyed the book, I'd be grateful if you post a short review on Amazon. Your feedback really makes a difference and helps others learn about my books. I appreciate your support!

Tonya Duncan Ellis

P.S. Please visit my website at www.tonyaduncan-ellis.com to see cool videos about Sophie and learn about upcoming books (I sometimes give away freebies!). You can also join Sophie's club to get updates about my new book releases and get a **FREE** gift.

Books by
Tonya Duncan Ellis

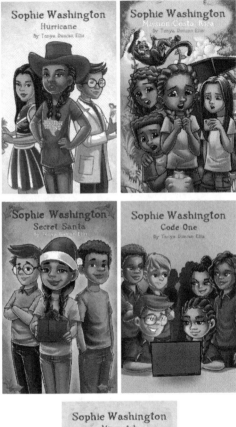

For information on all Tonya Duncan Ellis books about Sophie and her friends

Check out the following pages!

You'll find:

- Blurbs about the other exciting books in the Sophie Washington series

- Information about Tonya Duncan Ellis

Sophie Washington: Queen of the Bee

Sign up for the spelling bee?

No way!

If there's one thing ten-year-old Texan Sophie Washington is good at, it's spelling. She's earned straight one-hundreds on all her spelling tests to prove it. Her parents want her to compete in the Xavier Academy spelling bee, but Sophie wishes they would buzz off.

Her life in the Houston suburbs is full of adventures, and she doesn't want to slow down the action. Where else can you chase wild hogs out of your yard, ride a bucking sheep or spy an eight-foot-long alligator during a bike ride through the neighborhood? Studying spelling words seems as fun as getting stung by a hornet, in comparison.

That's until her irritating classmate, Nathan Jones, challenges her. There's no way she can let Mr. Know-it-All win. Studying is hard when you have a pesky younger brother and a busy social calendar. Can Sophie ignore the distractions and become Queen of the Bee?

Sophie Washington: The Snitch

There's nothing worse than being a tattletale...

That's what ten-year-old Sophie Washington thinks until she runs into Lanie Mitchell, a new girl at school. Lanie pushes Sophie and her friends around at their lockers and even takes their lunch money.

If they tell, they are scared the other kids in their class will call them snitches and won't be their friends. And when you're in the fifth grade, nothing seems worse than that. Excitement at home keeps Sophie's mind off the trouble with Lanie.

She takes a fishing trip to the Gulf of Mexico with her parents and little brother, Cole, and discovers a mysterious creature in the attic above her room. For a while, Sophie is able to keep her parents from knowing what is going on at school. But Lanie's bullying goes too far, and a classmate gets seriously hurt. Sophie needs to make a decision. Should she stand up to the bully or become a snitch?

Sophie Washington: Things You Didn't Know About Sophie

Oh, the tangled web we weave...

Sixth grader Sophie Washington thought she had life figured out when she was younger, but this school year everything changed. She feels like an outsider because she's the only one in her class without a cell phone, and her crush, new kid Toby Johnson, has been calling her best friend Chloe. To fit in, Sophie changes who she is. Her plan to become popular works for a while, and she and Toby start to become friends.

Between the boy drama, Sophie takes a whirlwind class field trip to Austin, Texas, where she visits the state museum, eats Tex-Mex food, and has a wild ride on a kayak. Back at home, Sophie fights off buzzards from her family's roof, dissects frogs in science class, and has fun at her little brother Cole's basketball tournament.

Things get more complicated when Sophie "borrows" a cell phone and gets caught. If her parents make her tell the truth what will her friends think? Turns out Toby has also been hiding something, and Sophie discovers the best way to make true friends is to be yourself.

Sophie Washington: The Gamer

40 Days Without Video Games? Oh No!

Sixth-grader Sophie Washington and her friends are back with an interesting book about having fun with video games while keeping balance. It's almost Easter, and Sophie and her family get ready to start fasts for Lent with their church, where they give up doing something for forty days that may not be good for them. Her parents urge Sophie to stop tattling so much and encourage her second-grade brother, Cole, to give up something he loves most—playing video games. The kids agree to the challenge but how long can they keep it up? Soon after Lent begins, Cole starts sneaking to play his video games. Things start to get out of control when he loses a school electronic tablet he checked out without his parents' permission and comes to his sister for help. Should Sophie break her promise and tattle on him?

Sophie Washington: Hurricane

#Sophie Strong

A hurricane's coming, and eleven-year-old Sophie Washington's typical middle school life in the Houston, Texas suburbs is about to make a major change. One day she's teasing her little brother, Cole, dodging classmate Nathan Jones' wayward science lab frog and complaining about "braggamuffin" cheerleader Valentina Martinez, and the next, she and her family are fleeing for their lives to avoid dangerous flood waters. Finding a place to stay isn't easy during the disaster, and the Washington's get some surprise visitors when they finally do locate shelter. To add to the trouble, three members of the Washington family go missing during the storm, and new friends lose their home. In the middle of it all, Sophie learns to be grateful for what she has and that she is stronger than she ever imagined.

Sophie Washington: Mission: Costa Rica

Welcome to the Jungle

Sixth grader Sophie Washington, her good friends, Chloe and Valentina, and her parents and brother, Cole, are in for a week of adventure when her father signs them up for a spring break mission trip to Costa Rica. Sophie has dreams of lazing on the beach under palm trees, but these are squashed quicker than an underfoot banana once they arrive in the rainforest and are put to work, hauling buckets of water, painting, and cooking. Near the hut they sleep in, the girls fight off wayward iguanas and howler monkeys, and nightly visits from a surprise "guest" make it hard for them to get much rest after their work is done.

A wrong turn in the jungle midway through the week makes Sophie wish she could leave South America and join another classmate who is doing a spring break vacation in Disney World.

Between the daily chores the family has fun times zip lining through the rainforest and taking an exciting river cruise in crocodile-filled waters. Sophie meets new friends during the mission week who show her a different side of life, and by the end of the trip she starts to see Costa Rica as a home away from home.

Sophie Washington: Secret Santa

Santa Claus is Coming to Town

Christmas is three weeks away and a mysterious "Santa" has been mailing presents to sixth grader Sophie Washington. There is no secret Santa gift exchange going on at her school, so she can't imagine who it could be. Sophie's best friends, Chloe, Valentina, and Mariama guess the gift giver is either Nathan Jones or Toby Johnson, two boys in Sophie's class who have liked her in the past, but she's not so sure. While trying to uncover the mystery, Sophie gets into the holiday spirit, making gingerbread houses with her family, helping to decorate her house, and having a hilarious ice skating party with her friends. Snow comes to Houston for the first time in eight years, and the city feels even more like a winter wonderland. Between the fun, Sophie uncovers clues to find her secret Santa and the final reveal is bigger than any package she's opened on Christmas morning. It's a holiday surprise she'll never forget!

Sophie Washington
Code One

Girl Power!

Xavier Academy is having a computer coding competition with a huge cash prize! Sixth grader Sophie Washington and her friend Chloe can't wait to enter with their other classmates, Nathan and Toby. The only problem is that the boys don't think the girls are smart enough for their team and have already asked two other kids to work with them. Determined to beat the boys, Sophie and Chloe join forces with classmates Mariama, Valentina, and "brainiac," Rani Patel, to form their own all-girl team called "Code One." Computer coding isn't easy, and the young ladies get more than they bargain for when hilarious mishaps stand in their way. It's girls versus boys in the computer coding competition as Sophie and her friends work day and night to prove that anything boys can do girls can do better!

Sophie Washington Mismatch

Watch out Venus and Serena, Sophie Washington just joined the tennis team, and she's on her way to becoming queen of the court!

That is until her coach matches her with class oddball, Mackenzie Clark, and the drama really begins...

Mackenzie refuses to talk to Sophie or learn the secret handshake she made up. Sophie just can't figure her out. Then Mackenzie starts skipping practice, and gets sick at school, and Sophie realizes that there's more to her doubles partner than meets the eye. Can Sophie make things right with Mackenzie before their first big game, or is their partnership a complete mismatch?

About the Author

Tonya Duncan Ellis is author of the Sophie Washington book series which includes: *Queen of the Bee, The Snitch, Things You Didn't Know About Sophie, The Gamer, Hurricane, Mission: Costa Rica, Secret Santa, Code One, Mismatch* and *My BFF*. When she's not writing, she enjoys reading, swimming, biking and travel. Tonya lives in Houston, TX with her husband and three children.